THE LIST

A SEEK AND FIND BOOK

b.b. cronin

PICNIC

VIKING

Today Grandad is taking
his grandchildren on a picnic.
But first he must tie the picnic basket
to the roof of his car.

Off they go!

Everyone cannot wait to get to the picnic grounds.

Especially since there are three delicious apples in the basket.

There are many different signs along the way.

But none of them says chocolate milk.

At a beautiful park, they decide to stop and look around.

But they do not eat the large watermelon slice from the basket.

They stop to take some pictures by a river

and think about the three big pretzels they will eat later.

Back in the car they go!

Now they are on the highway.

A banana would be a nice treat, but they'd better wait till the picnic.

In a small fishing village, a floating lifesaver makes the grandkids think of doughnuts.

There are two doughnuts in the basket. Grandad does not like doughnuts.

The village is full of shops. The grandchildren want to stop to get some cupcakes.

But Grandad already has three cupcakes in the basket.

There is a detour in the town, past a vegetable stand.

Corn on the cob is Grandad's favorite food.

Outside the town they need to stop to fill the car with gas.

There are signs for three kinds of ice cream cones: vanilla, chocolate, and lemon.

Finally they arrive at the picnic grounds.

Grandad is thinking of the cheese and lemonade he packed in the basket.

The picnic has fallen out of the basket along the drive.

Can you go back

to the start of their journey

and find all the items,

so Grandad and the kids

can have their picnic?

Mmmm . . .

Time

for a nap!

For my Mam and Dad

———

VIKING

An imprint of Penguin Random House LLC

375 Hudson Street

New York, New York 10014

First published in the United States of America by Viking,

an imprint of Penguin Random House LLC, 2017

LIBRARY OF CONGRESS CATALOGING-IN-PUBLICATION DATA IS AVAILABLE.

ISBN 9781101999226

1 3 5 7 9 10 8 6 4 2

Manufactured in China   Set in Brandon Text

Book design by Mark Melnick

The artwork for this book was rendered with acrylics on paper.